For Anne Hoppe, a great teacher
—L.M.S.

For Ruthie and Dennis
—S.K.H.

Follow Me, Mittens Text copyright © 2007 by Lola M. Schaefer Illustrations copyright © 2007 by Susan Kathleen Hartung All rights reserved. No part of this book may be used or reproduced in any manner whatsoever without written permission except in the case of brief quotations embodied in critical articles and reviews. Printed in the United States of America. For information address HarperCollins Children's Books, a division of HarperCollins Publishers, 1350 Avenue of the Americas, New York, NY 10019. www.harpercollinschildrens.com

Library of Congress Cataloging-in-Publication Data is available.
ISBN-10: 0-06-054665-4 (trade bdg.) — ISBN-13: 978-0-06-054665-6 (trade bdg.)
ISBN-10: 0-06-054666-2 (lib. bdg.) — ISBN-13: 978-0-06-054666-3 (lib. bdg.)

1 2 3 4 5 6 7 8 9 10 ❖ First Edition

I Can Read!

SHARED
My
First
READING

Follow Me, Mittens

story by **Lola M. Schaefer**

pictures by **Susan Kathleen Hartung**

■ HarperCollins*Publishers*

"Mittens," calls Nick.

"Let's go for a walk."

Meow! Meow!

"Follow me," says Nick.

Mittens follows Nick.

He follows Nick past trees.

He follows him over logs.
He follows Nick
into the flowers.

Mittens stops.

He smells a flower.

Flutter! Flutter!
A yellow butterfly
flies past Mittens.

It flies up, down,
and all around.

Flutter! Flutter!

Mittens follows the butterfly.

Flutter! Flutter!
The butterfly flies
around the bushes.
Mittens follows the butterfly.

Flutter! Flutter!

The butterfly flies over a rock.

Mittens follows the butterfly.

Flutter! Flutter!
The butterfly flies up, up,
and away.

Mittens cannot follow
the butterfly.

Mittens stops.

He looks all around.

Mittens cannot see Nick.

Mittens runs over the rock.

He runs around the bushes.

Mittens still cannot see Nick.

Meow! Meow!

"Mittens!" calls Nick.
Mittens hears Nick
call his name.

Mittens follows
the sound of Nick's voice.
Mittens runs and runs.

"MITTENS!"

MEOW!

Mittens sees Nick.

Mittens runs and jumps
into Nick's arms.

PURRRR! PURRRR!

"Follow me," says Nick.

Mittens follows Nick
all the way home.

25